Oh, no! Bob's phone keeps cutting off his words! Can you help Wendy figure out what he said? What do you see that starts with the letters

Aa , **Bb** , **Cc** , and **Dd** ?

When they get to the site, Bob calls again. "Look out for the **e**⚡ when you fix the **f**⚡ and the **g**⚡. I hope you brought a **h**⚡!"

Bob's cell phone is still cutting off his words. What begins with the letters

Ee , **Ff** , **Gg** , and

Hh ?

Hooray! The job is done! Back at Bob's home, Wendy's phone rings again. It's Bob! "I left the **i**〰 out next to the **j**〰 in the **k**〰! Is the **l**〰 there too?"

Can you help Wendy? What do you see that begins with

Ii , **Jj** , **Kk** , and

Ll ?

At lunchtime Bob calls again. "Did you remember to give Pilchard her **m**⚡?" he asks.

"By the way, if you need any **n**⚡, there are some on the table by the crate of **o**⚡ and the can of **p**⚡."

What did Bob say? Can you spot things that start with

Mm , **Nn** , **Oo** , and

Pp ?

Bleep-bleep! Wendy's cell phone rings. "Hi, it's me!" says Bob. "Thanks for taking my **q**⚡ to the cleaners. After you're done working on the **r**⚡, if you need the **s**⚡, it should be in my **t**⚡."

Can you find the things that begin with

Qq , **Rr** , **Ss** , and

Tt ?

"What's that?" asks Bob. "It's starting to rain? . . .

I hope you brought an **u**⚡. Be sure to cover up the **v**⚡

and the **w**⚡!"

What things do you see that begin with

Uu , **Vv** , and **Ww** ?

The rain has stopped, and now Scoop needs to dig a hole. Wendy calls Bob. "Sorry to bother you, but where should we dig?"

"You can't miss it!" Bob says. "**X**〜. Okay? **Y**〜."

What starts with **Xx** and **Yy**?